IN MEDIAS RES:
Stories from the In-Between

I0629691

John Dutterer	Ty Phelps
Paul Hostovsky	Barbara Ruth
Jennifer Stephan	Jyotsna Sreenivasan
Kapral	Paul Stansbury
L.C. Lara	Bonnie Jo
Sylvia J. Martínez	Stufflebeam
Jody T. Morse	Dorothy Tinker
Eloísa Pérez-Lozano	Alexis Vaughan
M. Kelly Peach	Christopher Walker

WRITESPACE

Copyrights

Contents

IN MEDIAS RES:
Stories from the In-Between

Editor's Note

HOLLY WALRATH

When we set out to create a second Writespace anthology over a year ago, we wanted to showcase the writing of the Houston community. In our second year, we knew we wanted to expand our anthology to beyond just Houston and Texas but still feature the kind of amazing, cross-genre work we see happening within our city. What we didn't realize is that our call would go not just beyond Texas, but beyond the borders of the United States—to places like Israel, Singapore, and Canada. We received submissions from across the globe, including: Australia, China, France, Germany, Guatemala, India, Israel, Japan, New Zealand, Pakistan, Poland, Scotland, and the UK. Only 20% of our submissions were from the state of Texas, out of over 200+ submissions. While it is amazing we managed to reach this far, and we are humbled by the international authors who loved our anthology theme enough to send us their work, it did mean we had to rework our ideas of how to approach accepting submissions for this year's anthology.

As the anthology editor, I feel transparency is tantamount. I admire editors like Neil Clarke of *Clarkesworld*, who served as Writefest's 2016 keynote speaker. If you're a reader of *Clarkesworld*, you know Neil is a numbers guy who loves to show who submitted, who was accepted, and gives good reasons why. That's why I'm going to give you a taste of the behind-the-scenes work of making this anthology, so you can see for yourself how we got this far.

We received over 200 submissions, a large number for our first open call. Those stories were stripped of their biographical and geographical markers. I then dropped them into a Google folder and shared them with our readers, a small team of dedicated Writespace volunteers who visited the folder, read stories, and rated them. After a first read, I stripped out the first round of stories based upon my own reading and the opinions of our readers. This dropped us down to about 100 stories. What made those first stories rejections? Some (less than 5%) simply did not fit the call for submissions. The majority of the problems with the stories we rejected in the first round had to do with readability, not theme.

The second round was much more exciting. We received so many great submissions. Writers really took the theme to heart and broke boundaries, either in structure or genre. On this level it came down to fine details—Did the story fit the theme? Did the story fulfill itself completely? How many submissions of similar content can we take? Finally, we perused the writers' backgrounds to make sure we weren't accepting multiple stories from one author and to consider location. When it came down to making cuts, highlighting a portion of authors from Texas took precedence. We made this decision for many reasons but primarily because the focus of our anthology is to support our growing community. I loved that we received so many international and outside of Texas submissions. I loved that we reached so many new people. But the anthology will be sold in Texas, to Texas writers, so supporting our local writing community came first. Perhaps one day we will consider an international anthology, and I know that our larger network would be able to make that happen. For now, we were forced to choose and support the writers close to home.

I believe strongly that the writers we selected are at the forefront of new, exciting stories in Houston and beyond. I am constantly amazed by how accepting this city is of new writers, and this anthology call only made more clear to me the idea that writing is a community on many levels. I'm thrilled to be able to expand our community further—beyond Houston, beyond Texas.

I'd like to thank everyone who sent a submission. Your work was read with great care and attention. Your willingness to send us your work astonishes us. I loved many stories we could not accept. It is my hope that next year we will be able to publish another anthology, and that we will receive even more great submissions. For now, I encourage you to keep submitting, keep writing, keep revising. Most importantly, keep reading!

Foreword

ELIZABETH WHITE-OLSEN

Writespace is growing. We always had dreams of embracing as wide of a range of writers as possible, but we never dreamed we would reach an international community. Though we're barely shy of being two years old, Writespace's expansion into an international community is already happening.

Along with representing geographical breadth themselves, the authors of the stories in this collection present readers with a great breadth of subject matter. From scarecrows to debate class to coyote conferences to a hearing man's longing to belong to the world of the Deaf, these stories explore what it means to be in worlds in-between—to worlds in-between reality and fantasy, between the status quo and the margins, between acceptance and solitariness.

The breadth of imagination demonstrated in the following pages is astounding. If you read these stories with an open heart, you will likely find yourself swiftly pulled into your own in-between state, into a state of "almost being there," present and amazed in one of these vibrant, alternate worlds. Whether you wake to find that your hand "has turned to steel" (Stufflebeam) or rise from the muck of the bayou to save a human jogger—and, in having been seen by her, realize you have "broken the one rule, cracking it in half like a crawfish and sucking out the middle" (Kapral)—or watched the liveliness of American Sign Language and discovered, alongside Paul Hostovsky's protagonist, that "ASL in the hands of Deaf people was—there's no other word for it—symphonic: the hands, face, eyebrows, eye-gaze, lips, tongue, head-tilt, shoulder-turn—all the various "sections" of the body's orchestra simultaneously creating meaning. A visual-gestural music rising up all at once like a controlled explosion" . . . you will find yourself stretched toward a new in-between that is incredibly expansive.

Thank you for supporting Writespace by purchasing this anthology. Through your purchase, you have helped Writespace further our mission of supporting writers of all genres develop their craft, careers, and confidence. Your engagement with our work and with these stories helps us to guide writers to break new boundaries and create new writing that excites the human spirit.

Stories are as important and yet sometimes as uncelebrated as the air we breathe. They have the unique power to build up or to tear down, to strengthen or to weaken, to deliver great happiness or leave great disappointment. These are the sorts of stories that build, strengthen, and deliver happiness, so enjoy them and let them accomplish their good work in you.

A Mexican-American Dandelion

ELOISA PEREZ-LOZANO

I'm a dandelion hair floating high above you, the brown, brown ground in this white, white world, not because I'm better but because I'm light and my words aren't caught in accents that get in the way of the words I say. And so the white winds pick me up with ease and toss me around because all they see are fuzzy gray wisps gripping at their gusts as my brown seed trails below me, ignored. Colored preconceptions blow past me down below as I glide in the gales, trying to express the culture they don't see when they look at me, the culture of brown, the one in my seed, but not in my skin, the skin that they see. The same skin that lets me linger here, blending into their air while you look up and yearn to fly with me, trying to be as light as you can, hoping to catch a breeze. I wish you would, because it's pretty lonely without more of our color shimmering, dancing in these whirling winds.

How to Get Over Your Fear of Public Speaking

SYLVIA J. MARTINEZ

Part I—Freshman Year

Sign up for Public Speaking your freshman year of high school because all the other electives will already be filled up. Go to the first class. Look at all the confident people in the room raise their hands when responding to the teacher about what topics might work for the first speech assignment. Notice none of the other students look like you. In fact, notice that most of your classmates are either white or Asian. Look down at your stiff, new white boots. Then look over at your classmate's nicer brown boots. They look comfortable, expensive. Cross your boots at your ankles and move them away from the nicer boots.

Focus on what is in front of you now. Count the silver ring spirals on your notebook while Jennifer Smith brings up speaking about recycling. Then count the horizontal blue lines on the paper while Ronald Wu suggests the topic of steroid use in baseball. Note the purple dot where the red vertical margin line meets the first horizontal blue line. Make this observation the purpose for your living at this moment. At all costs, avoid eye contact with Mr. Wendt. Decide while looking at the purple dot that this first class of public speaking is also your last.

Part II—Six Weeks Later

Get called into your counselor's office. Wonder why Dr. Young took so long to catch you but then remember three counselors and over 2,000 students probably has something to do with it. Eyeball the two worn-out seats she points to as she says, Have a seat, Clarissa. Pick the orange chair. Look toward the left wall at a poster of a bandana-headed woman mechanic flexing a muscle under a word bubble that says, "We Can Do It." Wonder what the "It" is supposed to be. Change a tire? Give someone an oil change? See that Dr. Young is still reading your file in silence as if you're not there. Then notice the framed University of California at Berkeley diploma on the wall behind her. Be impressed. Also see on the diploma that Dr. Young's whole name is Martha Jacqueline Young. Ponder the plausibility of her having had a nickname as a child, perhaps Marty or Little Martha? Picture Marty as a young black girl in school raising her hand with all the right answers. Wonder if she always wanted to be a high school counselor. Then let it dawn on you that she's the first minority you've spoken to face-to-face with a Ph.D. Realize something about the world is crooked from your vantage point.

Look at all the stacked boxes around a tall, grey metal shelf. Notice how the books on the shelf are stuffed anywhere they can fit. Glance at a few titles: *How to Get Into College; I'm Okay, You're Okay; The Souls of Black Folk.* So many books! Then look at piles of blue, green, yellow, and purple folders on the metal filing cabinet next to the overloaded coat rack in the corner. Wonder how someone with a Ph.D. from Cal can seem so disorganized!

Hear Dr. Young sigh. Try to peek at the purple file folder she has open in front of her because your name is on the tab: Garcia, Clarissa. Wonder if purple is code for freshman. Watch her close it as she sighs loudly again. Think about the word sigh. Question in your mind if it's onomatopoeic. Try to avoid smelling the coffee on her breath lingering from her second sigh. Coffee smells good firsthand, never secondhand. Feel the silence afterwards that you know she uses strategically to convey her disappointment in you. Listen to her with eye contact as she asks you, Are you planning on going to college, Clarissa? Resist the urge to contemplate whether this is a rhetorical question. It is not. Say yes because it's the right answer. Nod submissively when she informs you, Then you'll need to retake Public Speaking next fall.

Say, I will. (Mean it.)

Pick up your backpack and leave her office.

Forget about this meeting for several months.

Part III—Sophomore Year

Find yourself in the same classroom you were in before, the one where you counted silver spirals and blue lines and a red line and a purple dot. Be alert because this time the teacher will call you by name. Clarissa Garcia! How good to see you again! Listen as Mr. Wendt tells the whole class that the top three fears of Americans are public speaking, snakes, and confined spaces. Know, though, that he's really just talking to you. Wish at this moment that you were a snake in a confined space. But something about this image makes you remember Dr. Young's office, so pay attention this time.

Observe a new crowd of confident people talking about topics: teen pregnancy, alcoholism, and pesticides on fruit. Make a mental note to wash your apple later. Go back to your old way of avoiding eye contact: one blue line, two blue lines . . . Stop with a startle when Mr. Wendt taps his aged knuckle on your desk. And you, Clarissa? Any of these ideas sound interesting to you?

Don't think about writing a speech on teen pregnancy because, to you, that's not a topic. That's a fact of life for your oldest sister Olivia, who you love—and her baby boy, too. And besides, eighteen is officially adult status: She's a high school graduate with a job and still with the dad, and she's probably not the "teenage pregnancy" example people look for when writing a speech about teenage pregnancy. Also, don't think about speaking about alcoholism because that's the part of your father that makes you sad, which means you might end up crying during your speech and making it awkward for everyone. And don't speak on pesticides on fruit. Just don't. Instead, answer Mr. Wendt that you think you'll make your first speech on donating blood. Repeat yourself because he says he can't hear you. Feel pleased when he looks pleased with your repeated answer.

Prepare for your first speech by going to the San Francisco Mission Branch Public Library after school since the library is a beautiful place where you can concentrate. Check out books written by people from places like the Red Cross. Find more information in an encyclopedia in the B volume. Copy the information you find in the encyclopedia down in your notebook, because they don't let you check out reference books. Thank the librarian Susan for helping you find an article in a *Newsweek* about how safe it is to give blood, even with that AIDS virus going around. Think about calling your dad who works at a local blood bank now that he's retired from the Navy. Never get around to calling him, though. He's never home in the evenings when you call him, anyway. Write the speech on binder paper. Make the index note cards that Mr. Wendt requests the class use during speeches. In a week, deliver the speech by reading every word from the cards between your shaking hands, not looking up once.

Repeat this process four times. Get a C in the class. Feel relieved that it's over. Never again get called into Dr. Young's office.

Part IV—Untitled

Get into your first choice of colleges thanks to your hard work and Upward Bound's guidance. Take note of the look of negative surprise your creative writing teacher gives you when you tell her you got into Davis and four other great schools. Never forget that ugly look of disbelief on her face. You got an A on every assignment in her class, for crying out loud! Forget her name forever.

Part V—Freshman Year, Again

Look at the course offerings in the thick catalog the university sent you. Read the words "Recommended Electives for Freshmen: *Rhetoric and Communication 1*" (higher education's fancy way of saying "Public Speaking"). Feel your old fear creep up, but squash it and get brave. Sign up for the class again. This time speak loudly enough so that your voice is always clear and understood. Be the one raising your hand: hormones in milk, standardized tests, the importance of knowing Spanish in California, alcoholism. That's right, write on alcoholism this time—without crying. It's a disease, after all, and not your father. Look your audience in the eyes, pause when necessary, and only glance at your cards occasionally.

Get an A this time, and be proud of yourself.

Part VI—Conclusion

So you don't always look like the people around you. So what. You belong here, too.

The Cough

CHRISTOPHER WALKER

At around midnight it started. A rattling croak like stones in her chest ricocheting from rib to rib. She sat up in bed and the coughing began in earnest. My wife patted her on the back, but this did nothing. With every cough it sounded as though she was trying to disgorge her lungs. It was sickening to hear, a rough, abrasive sound that belonged to a dying animal, not my two-year-old daughter.

"She's not stopping," my wife said.

"So what do we do?" I asked. Tears were streaming down my daughter's face, her cheeks turning beet red, her forehead a remarkable alabaster white from the severity of her effort. Her face was like the Polish flag.

My wife's voice rang with panic. I was always the clear, cool head in an emergency but only because we'd never had a serious one until that moment. Kinga had thrown up in bed once, wet it twice, but otherwise these early years had been blessed. The remedy for most sleepless nights was simple and easily applied: a soothing gel to treat the gums as they were pierced by the latest new tooth. Such tribulations seemed petty now compared to a cough that threatened imminent suffocation.

I tried to get Kinga to drink. She took in a mouthful, but swallowing was out of the question and soon her pyjamas and the bedsheets were damp from the regurgitated water. Katarzyna was out of the bed by this stage, tossing clothes around in a desperate search for something in which to dress Kinga.

Where are we going?" I asked.

"To the night hospital," my wife said.

I dressed Kinga as well as I could, given her alarmed state. She seemed not quite conscious of what was happening. She looked at me with her large, brown, watery eyes, as if to ask why I wasn't doing something to help her.

I wrapped her up in a thick, fur-lined coat, her hands disappearing inside the cuffs. Then I opened both windows in the bedroom as wide as they would go and lifted my daughter up so that she could breathe in the crisp night air. She felt so light in my arms, and in the cold she trembled like a leaf in a storm. Her coughing eased.

"How are we getting to this hospital?" I asked Katarzyna when she reappeared.

"My brother's coming over. He'll be here in ten minutes, but I have to go down and adjust the car seat."

"Are we taking his car or ours?"

"Ours," Katarzyna said. There was an edge to her voice that suggested I'd asked a stupid question. I sensed trouble, perhaps conflict. Whenever there was something important to do, my wife disappeared into the far reaches of her mind and cut me out entirely. I was always left with just the pieces to pick up and examine, like a monkey trying to assemble a jigsaw puzzle.

Her brother looked sleepily at us when he arrived and complained about how he had a university lecture to go to at nine. Katarzyna spoke to him harshly in Polish. I wondered why and wished I could have followed the thread of her thoughts—it looked to me so much like we were in her brother's debt and yet there she was haranguing him.

Kinga's cough abated, the occasional rumblings issuing now like aftershocks following a shallow earthquake.

Katarzyna lost her temper with the car seat. She blamed her brother, who borrowed our car a week previously to go and visit friends in Krakow. I kept my lips sealed as I stood there, sleepy Kinga resting her head on my shoulder. I'd never understood why we bought the car, and when Katarzyna and I argued, the car often came up. I'd previously given her the money to buy one and for her to have driving lessons, but she'd spent the money on other so-called essentials. When some cousins offered us their old Fiat at a good price, I'd had to pay all over again. We'd had the car for three years, and all we had to show for our purchase was three years' worth of insurance bills. My advice, that we ought to wait until we were confident, competent drivers, had been ignored in favour of Katarzyna's parents' encouragement. The conversations we'd had were not gratifying, and I'd felt increasingly pushed to the periphery as the negotiations continued apace without me.

I was often left rueing my lack of Polish.

The night hospital was on the other side of the city. There was no traffic to speak of, so we made good time. Kinga fell asleep in the car seat, snoring soundly as we skimmed along on the tarmac.

12

She coughed once or twice, but her two doses of fresh air had had a restorative effect.

We pulled into a small car park by a long squat building. I could just discern in the gloom the signs that announced that this was a medical facility. Katarzyna's brother said he'd stay in the car and wait, though Katarzyna warned that we could be hours. I lifted Kinga out of the seat and her arms instinctively curled around my neck. Her warm breath played over my skin. She was contentedly asleep.

The floor inside the building was sticky underfoot, though why it should have been so, I couldn't discern. There were none of the decorative flora and fauna of the English emergency room: no victims of violent crime, no trail of blood or urine. The floor was sticky because no one bothered to run a mop over it.

At the little registration window, two glum faces peered up at Katarzyna as she explained our problem. One of them looked past her at the silent form of my daughter in my arms, gave a shrug, and pointed down to the end of the corridor.

It was dim, with only half of the lights turned on to throw down their sickly cool glare on the ceramic tiles along the wall and floor. Posters glued to the walls were peeling at the corner and advertised medicine a decade old. Hopeless faces looked up at us as we made our way in the direction of the room we had been sent to.

Katarzyna asked the crowd in the waiting room who was last. This was the Polish system, and it worked well enough if you were Polish and had the ability to announce yourself. I preferred the more introverted English system, wherein everyone in the queue had a numbered card which they hung on the wall when they were called to see the doctor. You didn't have to speak to your fellow patients in my home country; here, you had no choice.

The waiting room was crowded and there was nowhere to sit. I observed the gathered throng of parents with their sick children. We were in the infant department, it seemed, as there were no drunks with broken noses here, no elderly patients with heart palpitations, only children with rashes streaming sorely up their throats, hacking coughs that sent shivers down their backs with every new expulsion, the dried crimson of a lately bloody nose.

I felt a wave of heat rising up through my body. It was winter and I was wearing a coat able to sustain a living organism in temperatures well below freezing, Fahrenheit or Centigrade. The waiting room was broiling me like a piece of meat in the oven, but Katarzyna looked as though mentally she were somewhere else as she sorted through her books of notes and old prescriptions. When I asked her to take Kinga from me so I could remove my coat, she acted as if she hadn't heard.

One after another the parents disappeared with their offspring into the little room across the corridor. There'd be the sound of crying, or sometimes wailing, and then they'd exit with a mumbled *"do widzenia"* and a disconsolate look etched into their faces.

Soon it was our turn. Katarzyna ushered me and Kinga into the room, trying to rouse our daughter as she stripped off her coat and top. Kinga groaned and began to cry. She was too young to explain anything to, though I tried, anyway, hoping that my level voice would placate her.

Katarzyna started speaking to the doctor, who had yet to turn from his computer and look at us. He was a fine specimen. He was dressed in grey slacks and an off-white t-shirt two sizes too big for his arms, but only just big enough to contain his burgeoning stomach. His thin hair was slick against his liver-spotted scalp, a thin film of sweat greasing his skin. He wore glasses, which he took off now to clean with the end of his t-shirt. He stretched out an arm and took from Katarzyna the documents she had brought, and then he copied some of the information onto his computer, typing slowly with his two forefingers—press a letter, check the screen, press a letter, check the screen. His head shook from side-to-side to say perhaps that he was too busy concentrating on his secretarial duties to listen to my wife's diatribe, or to say that her concerns were none of his and she was acting the typical mother, blowing everything out of proportion.

He diagnosed everything without once looking at Kinga, who now rested on Katarzyna's lap, eyes half-open and her head lolling as though she had been sedated. Katarzyna said something in response to his diagnosis, and the doctor grunted. He stood and approached, flicking Kinga's top up to reveal her bare chest; he pressed the business end of his stethoscope against the skin, but it was clear he was doing this more to shut Katarzyna up than to honour Hippocrates. Only one of the ear buds on the stethoscope was where it belonged, the other hanging limply by his cheek.

He spoke some more and made some notes on a prescription pad. I asked Katarzyna what he was saying, and she ignored me. He took something out of a small fridge kept by his desk—it was a vial, and into this, he stuck the point of a needle. He filled the thin syringe with a clear liquid. I asked Katarzyna what it was, and now she acknowledged my question with a dismissive wave of the hand.

The doctor brought the needle over, and Katarzyna rolled up Kinga's sleeve. The doctor used a wet cotton wool pad to moisten and hopefully sterilise the skin, and with no further preamble, the needle passed into Kinga's triceps. She moaned, her eyes opened wide and when she saw what was happening she launched into an extended howl. This cry broke apart, becoming a deep, roaring, almost asthmatic cough, her symptoms suddenly returning in full force. But by now the doctor had grown tired of our visit and was already calling out for the next patient.

We dressed Kinga in the corridor, and I did my best to calm her. I shushed and rocked her and soon she fell asleep again.

As we left the night hospital, I asked Katarzyna why she hadn't translated the doctor's words for me.

"There wasn't time," she said.

"What do you mean 'there wasn't time'?" I said, trying not to raise my voice beyond a whisper.

"Don't raise your voice," she said, and that's where the conversation concluded. We woke up her brother, loaded Kinga's sleeping form into the back of the car, and returned home.

It was a whole day until Katarzyna thought to tell me what the injection had been, and even then she only told me in Polish. The translation I found offered four equivalent terms, and I didn't know how to choose between them.

Kinga's cough never returned, and in the morning she acted as if she had slept uninterrupted through the night.

Matrices

ALEXIS VAUGHAN

Grandmother

A woman who needs control, I get what I want. You tell me what to do because I give it all to you. You are all that I want. You are north south east west, and the way to have you in this world is to bow down. So I do. I win you. I play meek. I keep you. I give you three boys. I gain ground, I gain confidence, I tell you what to do. All my desire, my ambition, must be realized through you. Depending what sort of man you are, you could a) utterly cave and let me rule, becoming a shell of yourself, though you occasionally lash out b) push back from your own self worth and come to know mine. Appreciate it, use it. Ours could be akin to a true partnership. Or, c) you leave me. Unmanned, you experience this as your personal shame, a thing you should have extinguished: your woman imagines she can rule. You. Or anything. In a world without you, I don't know who I am, so I never let you go, though you're gone. The rest of my life I obsess, alone. Still each day I get up and cut the crust from my bread and nothing, goddammit, nothing, gets me down. Think what I could do with freedom.

Mother

Growing up I was forbidden to eat peanut butter and chocolate milk, a medical hex to keep acne away. No facial scarring would stand between me and the boy who felt me up at age twelve in a closet. This happened too young, though I won't tell my daughters quite when. I say it's for their own good. Really, I have cut her off, that little girl in the closet who knows the details of who, what, when, and how many times. My girls are my treasures, and they become my offering, when one day I meet a man who wants me under his thumb. I like it. I decide to give it my all: ah, this shall be my masterpiece. All inspiration, all purpose, my calling, my very soul will be to study torment with this man. And one by one, my children flee. My heart becomes an echo chamber for their rejection, their survival cries. Why can't they see the beauty of this enterprise? To encompass all life, all death, daily: fed by the teaspoon, dogged by the whip, True Love always a dangling possibility. It is a gorgeous sacrifice to cut the fruit of your womb from your heart and dash them on the rocks: See? You don't really know me.

Survivor

I will save them. It is for my girls I left behind my house and my Love. We were so in love. He saved me. When my father died, he was there to catch me—when I lost my compass and fell and fell and fell into his arms. I thought, this must be it: life as it is born in us to live. Soon after I was pregnant. With the first one, then the next. His earplugs in, he never heard our babies' cries, though I rose every time. Alone in my own home, I would not let them cry alone. He wanted a third. Can't we try for a boy? Outside my window a cat in heat screams: Did you know the feline penis has spines? Our third comes. It's a girl! Holding the tiny thing, in tableau with her sisters, he says: "I have so many girls!" I glimpse this moment of fatherly pride, performed for visiting family, as I am wheeled to the O.R. to be stitched. Years later, the memory winks at me as he rips the bathroom door from its hinges. I am an educated woman, I'm supposed to know how to get out of this. I take a recording of our fights to an attorney. My tinny, digital voice, screaming, takes me apart from myself. Oh, this is a scalding enterprise.

Reformer

I believe in equality, but no man is my equal. Just think: I know as much as you do, yet more, because my experience is richer, as one oppressed. Nevertheless, I'm grateful to live in times like these. If you please, I no longer bow. I envision, I shape, I build. I am never directionless. Arguably, I am foremost in my field, when I select a life partner and choose motherhood. Daughter! The word pit-pats through an inner space of egoless purpose, unleashing some new force. I thought I believed in altruism, but this is a thing beyond. I find a harrowing significance in the relationship between a feminist father and his daughter, her self-worth deepened by his regard. I will do anything to support this: the love of my man for our girl, the solidity of our partnership a demonstration, for her, of healthy wholeness. Are we acting? In the practiced fairness of our love, what lurks that can't be untaught, that has me still on tip-toe? He needs my adoration, but I need his just as much. I'm just better at living without it. I can do without anything: recognition, wealth, the enterprise I rise daily to build. Let it all fall. Just, please, may She thrive. Motherhood has always been a kind of sublimation.

Virgin

Mother, your love has its poison. I take it all in and have to spit some out. We sit at dinner, brothers and sisters breaking bread. You hold his hand as he smashes the table with the other one, because I want to go to a dance. Full of sex and spit and fear and revelation, I am 13 years old. I have no direction, I don't know what's happening to me, that's supposed to be your job. The back of my tongue has a gospel to sing, but it's stuck: when I try to make music all that comes out is bile. I am caught retching into the toilet after meals. You fear pregnancy: I haven't even had my period yet. You confront me: a girl with rebellion in her heart, what isn't she capable of? There are whores and there are virgins, and in white panic, I see what you truly think of me. My mind narrows to a grim, gray half-light, and now I know: This is about power. No: you are the tainted one, because you give yourself to That Man. As for me, I shall become this church inside myself. I emerge from the bathroom a serene supreme being that no man may touch; only I decide what goes in and out of my body. My body is my temple, my convent, my enterprise. The last stand of the utterly powerless is hunger.

Artist

My potential is intoxicating; everyone thinks so. I am of sound mind and body and the wind is at my back: What endeavor of mine can fail? And the world seems open to us. Women. More and more there are female faces, female voices, within the visible power structure. I toil my days away in pursuit: convert or kill, goes the battle cry. By night, though. Dark uprisings from the uncharted within: against my will, my agile, dreaming mind works it out, sets the record straight. All of recorded history has been lived under patriarchy. This inherited imbalance of power means wounds: We are not whole, we are not healed, not one of us. Anyone knows this, who seeks to know. And yet this truth, this art, in me: it is a repressed unknowable. Push it down. Who am I to turn this ship around? My world cannot stomach this knowledge; it must not take any shape that has my name. We dare not acknowledge mystery even if nothing, quite literally nothing, begins without Her begetting, and no one finds home but by Her cardinal points. I wake and chase the dream again, bowing to extrinsic valuation. I aim to please no one, if not Our Eternal Father.

19

Deaf Date

PAUL HOSTOVSKY

She was my sign language teacher. It wasn't until the end of the semester that I'd finally learned enough signs to ask her out. And even then I wasn't sure if I'd asked her out on a DATE or on a DESSERT, because they're homonyms, two signs that look the same but have different meanings. There are lots of these homonyms in sign language: SOCKS/STARS, EXPERT/BALLSY, HATE/GREAT, LOYAL/LAZY, the number 9 and the letter F. It's a foreign language. Except that it's domestic.

As it turned out, it was both a date and a dessert. We went to a coffee place that served pastries. She drove.

I didn't even know that Deaf people were allowed to drive. I would have thought it was illegal. Which it was, she said, up until the 1940s when the National Association of the Deaf convinced lawmakers that Deaf drivers posed no threat to public safety. Driving is essentially a visual act, she said as we got into her Toyota, and according to statistics, Deaf people make better drivers than hearing people. At least that's what I think she said. I nodded and smiled a lot without entirely understanding her. There's a sign in ASL for nodding and smiling without understanding: DINOSAUR-NOD. It means to feign understanding. I did a lot of that. Putting the car in drive, she asked if I'd like to listen to the radio.

It seemed rude to listen to the radio while sitting there next to her. Sort of like watching a strip-tease while sitting next to a blind person. So I said NO THANKS, which looks the same as NO GOOD. The sign for NO GOOD can also be done in shorthand with just the letters NG, like that Chinese surname, Ng, which I never know how to pronounce. The grammar of ASL is closer to Chinese than English, say the linguists. And pronunciation in ASL is all about the four parameters: handshape, movement, location, palm orientation. A slight mispronunciation, with the wrong palm orientation, can mean the difference between GRAD SCHOOL and SEXUAL INTERCOURSE.

You can't learn ASL from a book, she had told our class. You have to learn it from Deaf people. Because it belongs to Deaf people. And it belongs with Deaf people. Hearing people think they can go out, buy a book, and learn sign language on their own, apart from Deaf people. But they can't. If you try to learn from a book, she said, you end up signing like a book: stiff, flat, square. And who wants to be a square? Deaf people won't understand you. And you won't understand them.

The best way to learn ASL, she said, is to MIX with Deaf people. You have to FRATERNIZE with Deaf people. The sign for FRATERNIZE is a thumbs-up and a thumbs-down, mixing. And so I took her injunction to heart: I asked her out on a date. I wanted to mix with her, to fraternize with her. The date, as it turned out, was both thumbs-up and thumbs-down.

The thumbs-up part was having her all to myself for a whole hour. She was hot. She was no longer the teacher standing in front of the class, her butt singing to me when she turned to write on the blackboard. Now it was just the two of us sitting across from each other, nibbling our pastries, sipping our coffees.

It's HOT, she signed above the cup. I nodded and smiled. She pursed her lips and blew a ripple across the tiny pond of her latte. I knew the sign for HOT. I wondered if there was another, separate sign for HOT in the sensual sense, the sexual sense. I wanted to ask her about that, but she was doing most of the talking—most of the signing—and I couldn't get a word in edgewise, except for my old standby, the DINOSAUR-NOD.

She was very animated. Her face was more alive than any face I had ever seen. Her eyes, her eyebrows, her mouth, the tilt of her head. All the tiny muscles in her face. They were all so expressive. I wanted to tell her how animated she was, but I didn't know the sign for ANIMATED. I knew only that in English it comes from the Latin *anima*, which means soul or life force. I knew also that when conversing with a Deaf person in sign language you look at their face, which holds most of the meaning, only taking their hands in peripherally.

The thumbs-down part was, while watching her face for meaning, I kept thinking how animated and hot she was, and how distracting it all was—how it distracted me from what she was saying. So I did a lot of smiling and nodding and feigned my understanding. And when she caught me doing it she accused me right on the spot: YOU DINOSAUR-NOD ME. It was an indictment. And I was guilty as charged.

Guilty as charged, I wanted to tell her, but I didn't know how to sign AS CHARGED. I only knew GUILTY. So I signed it, smiling sheepishly. But she said I shouldn't feel guilty. I just shouldn't do it anymore. She told me to speak up, interrupt her, tell her when I didn't understand. Because, she said, saying you understand when you don't is rude in Deaf culture. It's dishonest. It's the cardinal sin. And Deaf people can tell when you've committed it.

And for a while I did speak up. I interrupted her a few times to ask: WHO? And more often than not she answered: ME! Because although the objects and verbs of her sentences were plain enough, it was often the subjects that gave me the most trouble. They were elusive, especially when she herself was the subject. She seemed to omit the first person as though it were understood. Maybe for Deaf people it is understood. But for me, it wasn't.

I had always been good at languages. I studied French and German in high school and college. I think this gave me an advantage when I began learning ASL because, as it turns out, French and ASL are related, historically speaking, etymologically speaking. For example, they both use the verb HAVE to express being (*il y'a*). And being with her now, I realized I wanted to have her. I also vaguely wanted to be her. Being and having became conflated.

I wasn't interested in getting an A. And I wasn't interested in being an interpreter—she had told me once, with more study, I might become an interpreter. But what I really wanted, I began to see, looking her full in the face and taking in all the grammar there, all the *anima* there, taking her hands in peripherally, fluent as chopsticks, was this: I wanted to be Deaf.

Capital D Deaf. Which had nothing to do with not hearing. And everything to do with seeing. Above all else, I wanted to see. And to belong. To be a citizen of the Deaf world, that vast network of cousins-once-removed that was the Deaf community; that warm, hugging, concrete, candid physicality that was the Deaf culture. I didn't want to be just a visitor or a guest anymore, a tourist, an interloper, an anthropologist. I wanted to belong there, to share that connection I knew she had with her Deaf friends, the ones I saw her chatting with after class in the cafeteria, their hands flitting, darting, flying, their faces alive, their signs as noiseless as their laughter was loud.

Watching them, it occurred to me that ASL in the hands of Deaf people was—there's no other word for it—symphonic: the hands, face, eyebrows, eye-gaze, lips, tongue, head-tilt, shoulder-turn—all the various "sections" of the body's orchestra simultaneously creating meaning. A visual-gestural music rising up all at once like a controlled explosion.

To me, it wasn't linear, not the way English is—one discrete word following on the heels of the next like a line of ponderous elephants trudging along. I wanted to be Deaf, which meant I didn't want to be ponderous and discrete anymore. I wanted to fly. To blend. I wanted to see and be and create the music, the explosion, the way only Deaf people could do.

She'd told the class it was considered a great compliment when a Deaf person says, YOU SIGN LIKE DEAF. And if they mistake you for a Deaf person, that was the greatest compliment of all. Yes, I wanted to be Deaf. And across the table, at that small coffee shop in the midst of that moment, that's what I confessed: ME WISH DEAF ME.

She smiled at that. It was a big, sad, beautiful smile. She was pretty and sweet and animated, and I had been emboldened to tell her, to confide in her, that I wished I could be like her; that somewhere deep inside me, I wished I were Deaf. She looked right at me then, long and hard, as though searching my face for something—something pure, simple, limpid, liquid, fragile, perishable, maybe even hazardous—and not finding it there, wrapped a delicate hand around her latte, which had surely grown cold, raised the half-empty cup into the air, and, as if toasting me, said: JUST BE YOURSELF.

The Mirror

JYOTSNA SREENIVASAN

I'm lying on this hard hospital delivery bed with only a small thin robe over my body. My legs, even my knees, are all uncovered and my bare feet are in these "stirrups," they call them. It's indecent, how you must be to give birth. In India do they cover the women more? I don't know, but here in America no one cares, they go about in shorts and swimming suits anyway, even the old fat ladies do it, exposing all their white wrinkled flesh just like that.

My hands and arms are cold. My stomach is a big mountain. Every so often it gets hard and I know I'm having a contraction. It doesn't hurt at all. They gave me a shot in my back, an "epidural," they call it. I'm glad. I was afraid I would scream and embarrass myself.

The American nurse comes in. She's thin and tall. She wears a short white skirt and white stockings and white shoes and a white cap. She smiles. I have gotten used to these Americans smiling all the time. When I first came here in April of 1963, almost two years ago, I thought, why are they always laughing at me? At first I thought, it's my sari and my kumkum. They have never seen someone wearing a sari and kumkum before. Then, after I took off the kumkum and began wearing skirts and shaving my legs and everything, still they laughed. I thought, what's wrong with me, that they should be showing their teeth every time I appear? Maybe it's because I'm brown, I thought. But they have seen brown people before. There are plenty of these Africans everywhere— "Negroes," they call them—and yet they, too, would laugh at me. I could not understand it. Finally I asked my friend Mary Pryor. She's my closest friend in America. She is a single lady and she owns a house and we stay in the apartment in the basement. Imagine, a single lady owning her own house and even renting it to strangers!

Mary told me, "Prema, they are not laughing at you. They are just being friendly. You must also smile when you meet someone."

My husband isn't here yet. He's a resident doctor at this hospital and that's why he will be allowed to be with me at the birth. He's just finishing up some work and he'll be here soon.

Otherwise, I would have to be all alone. I'm glad I will not be all alone.

In India, I would have my baby in the "nursing home" near my mother's house. That's what they call the places where ladies go to have babies—"nursing homes." The place is just two streets from my mother's house. It's in the home of a doctor—a lady doctor, of course. In India, they don't have men doctors for ladies. But here they think nothing of having a man look at that part of a lady and put his fingers in and everything. Thoo! It's disgusting. But what to do? Here I am in America.

My elder sister went to this nursing home last year to have her baby, and I still have not seen my first niece. I don't know when we will go back home. Sometimes I wonder, why did I agree to marry a man who wanted to study in America? I thought it would be fun to come here. I saw pictures of American homes in magazines and everything looked so nice, so clean. When I was a little girl, I thought, people in America must not ever use the toilet. I could not imagine such large white people ever needing to do something dirty like that. It's funny what children think about.

"How're we doing, Mrs.—" The nurse looks at a piece of paper on a clipboard. "How d'you say your name?"

"Mrs. Venkatesh," I say. "I am fine, thank you." I smile a little bit. I am too cold to smile very much.

The nurse pushes up my robe and puts her fingers in down there. This is the part I hate about having a baby, having everyone feeling around down there. "Good," she says. "Eight centimeters. When you start pushing, I can adjust this mirror so you can see." She points to a round mirror above the bed.

"See what?"

"So you can see the baby coming out!" she exclaims.

"Oh. No. No." Then I remember my manners. "No, thank you." Only in America would they have something so the woman can see! What is there to see? It's bad enough to have all this happening down there, in that part of my body. But what can I do? God made us give birth from there. Don't ask me why. Seeing isn't going to help anything.

The nurse leaves the room. I don't know where my husband is. At the time I agreed to come to America, I had no idea what it would really be like. When I first arrived here in Akron, Ohio, there were no leaves at all on the trees. I thought, so America is like this, with no leaves on the trees, no flowers. I have come from India, which is full of flowers, to this God-forsaken place. I was so unhappy. Before I arrived, I thought, my husband is a doctor, and we will be going to the richest country in the world. I will live like a queen. I didn't know the hospital did not pay residents well. I didn't know we would have to live in a basement apartment with paint and everything falling off the ceiling. I didn't know we would not be able to find basic Indian groceries, not even dal or ghee or yogurt. At home we have a cook and I never learned to make my own ghee or yogurt. Here I somehow make something or other using split peas and corn oil and sour cream. My mother sends me spices every so often, sambar powder and rasam powder, but I cannot find fresh chilies or coriander leaves. The only coconut in the store here is dried and sweetened, so I cannot use it. Imagine, eating South Indian food without coriander leaves or coconut!

But it's not so bad. I am used to it now. The main thing was, I was bored. My husband was at the hospital all day and even at night sometimes. I don't drive and, anyway, where would I go? There is only one other Indian couple near us and both of them, husband and wife, are doctors, so they are both just as busy. How to spend my time? Besides cooking and cleaning, I did some knitting and I went upstairs to watch TV with Mary. Finally one day I said to my husband, let's have a baby. My mother is writing asking why we are not expecting yet. I need some way to spend my time. Let's have a baby.

So here I am in the hospital. The nurse comes in again and checks me. "Ten centimeters," she says. "You're ready." The doctor is here now, a man doctor. He's wearing a mask and is pulling on some rubber gloves.

The nurse puts her hand on my stomach. "OK, push now," she says. So every time I feel my stomach tighten, I push as hard as I can.

"Good!" the nurse says. "I can see the head. Are you sure you don't want to see?"

I put my elbows on the bed and try to sit up. I want to see my baby.

"Lie down," she says. "You can't see that way. You need to use the mirror."

"Yes," I say. "Yes, I want to see." My heart is going thump-thump-thump so fast.

The nurse pulls the mirror down and I can see something, a shiny black-haired head. I can see what the man doctor is seeing. I don't care that he is seeing that part of me. I want to see my baby's face.

"Push," the nurse says.

I hold my breath and push. I can see the head come out. The face is turned the other way.

"Good," says the doctor. "Push again."

I see the rest of the body slide out and the doctor catches it. "It's a girl!" he says.

A girl. I had wanted a boy first and then a girl next. I wanted a big brother who would protect his younger sister. But I have a girl! I thank God. Anyway, my older brother never protected me. A girl is good. I hold out my arms and try to sit up. "Let me see her."

The nurse laughs. "So you wanted to see, after all. I'll clean her off."

I don't want to wait. Just then, my husband arrives. I had forgotten about him. "A girl!" I shout to him. "There she is."

He peeks over the nurse's shoulder. I'm jealous that he gets to see her first, when I'm the one who's been carrying her. "Bring her here," I say.

He brings her to me all wrapped up tight in a white blanket. Only her face shows. I try to sit up and take her, but the doctor, who's still doing something down there, says, "Lie still!"

So I can only look. Her black eyes look at me. "She's so white!" I exclaim. "Why is she so white?" I wonder if this is one more thing I didn't know about America—that babies born here turn white.

"It's okay," my husband says. "Even Indian babies are white when they're first born."

I look at her dark eyes and dark hair. I touch her cheek with one finger and she turns her mouth towards my finger. "She thinks it is food!" I say. "What, are you my American baby?" I ask. "I saw you come out in that round mirror," I tell her. "Here in America, they have things like that, so Amma can see you right away."

Middle Stream

JODY T. MORSE

In the Middle.

Squished between everybody else. Never the beginning, the first. Never the end, the last. My mother is a middle child. Is she better for it or was being in the middle a detriment? We sleep in the middle of a sleeping bag, between the zipped covers. Twinkies conceal a sugary goo treasure in the middle. Will the middle live forever like Twinkies? July is the middle month, always providing us the fifteenth—usually a good middle day. People get paid. You're headed toward the end but still have plenty of time to finish.

Middle of the pack.

Safety in numbers. Stay close to the center of the herd, little lamb, and you'll be safe from the wolves. Marathoners. Start in the middle, and then sprint at the end to win. The middle fork at a place setting, sandwiched between the salad and dessert fork, is used to eat the entree. It should be the strongest, biggest fork. The meatiest, even for a vegetarian like me. Middle of the road. Figuratively and literally. Why did the chicken cross the road? To pass through the middle. You can't get to the end without passing through the middle. Full of chaos and turmoil and change. In a story the middle is the climax, a point of high tension. The peak of the roller coaster mountain. The rest is downhill. Being brought to conclusion. One little, two little, three little Indians. Two Indians. Are these Indians from America or India? In my childhood, America. In my daughter's, India. Middle America. The Midwest. Where I grew up, Kentucky. Where exactly does the Midwest begin and end? Middle-aged. That has changed. Used to be thirty. Then forty. Now fifty-plus. People live longer—the middle has moved. *Malcolm In The Middle.* I never watched that show but for some reason I recognize the name Frankie Muñoz. That was the kid's name, right? Middlesex. Who in their right mind names a town Middlesex?!? Of all of the words in the English language, that's what you go with for the name of your town? Seriously, people, come on. At least give a median effort. Balancing in the middle. On a teeter-totter, the safest place is in the middle. There you don't get thwacked on the ground or launched too high into the sky. Fork in the middle of the road—take the left or the right. If you don't, you might hit a tree or a statue or a well-groomed flower bed.

You've reached the midway point.

I don't know if this is the midway point—not until I count the words on the page. Mid-sentence. Sometimes ideas pop into my head mid-sentence. There I am talking or typing and, all of a sudden, BAM! I'm hit with a flying notion. Then, I'm stuck. Do I finish the conversation or prose risking loss of the interrupting thought or stop what I'm doing or saying to write it down? Interrupting cow. Love that joke! Medium. A version of middle. A medium can read your thoughts, see the future or connect you with a dead relative, supposedly. I'm a bit skeptical about their powers and the use of the word "medium" to describe them. But I guess they are "in the middle"—between the living and the dead and the past and present.

Marginal.

No, that M word is not like the others—middle, median, medium. Close, but no cigar—marginal. Thanks for playing. Meddle is one letter off from middle. You want to be in the middle of something, if you tend to meddle. Someone I'm grateful meddled in my life is my midwife. Had it not been for her, my daughter might have died right there in the birthing tub. Melanie was definitely a middle, the connection between my daughter living and dying. The middle between me and her. Metacarpal? Nope. Well, maybe. Hmm. Is the prefix *"meta-"* related to middle? Where's my Latin dictionary and my anatomy book? On the middle bookshelf, of course. That's the best place for them. Don't want the shelves to be top-heavy. And these books are heavy! But at the bottom, I wrench my back picking them up. So, middle is best for keeping the shelf and me upright. Medium heat. Hot sauce from Taco Bell. Not Fire but not Mild. Where does Verde fall on the spicy-heat spectrum? I don't like spicy foods. They give me gas and heartburn. I'll stick with Mild, if you don't mind. Mid-sized sedan—sensible vehicle. Unless you live in the desert sands or swamp lands. Then a mid-sized sedan is not your best choice. Not even close.

In the midst.

Another way to say "in the middle." As in, "in the midst of the misty marsh . . ." There's a tongue-twister. Say that five times fast! Can middle be a state of mind? I'm having a middle day. Meaning, I'm not too happy or too sad, too busy or too lax. I'm going to start using that phrase. Be a trend setter. It's a "middle day" for me today.

I find myself in the middle of it all.

Two Old Friends in the Garden

M. KELLY PEACH

It was an ideal day for gardening—warm, but not too warm, because of the nice breeze blowing in from the north. Sunny, but not too sunny, because of the veil of hazy clouds high in the sky. Tim had spent the morning planting several rows of acorn squash, pumpkins, and green peppers in his quarter-acre vegetable garden. With that chore finished he could begin waging the summer-long war against weeds every gardener fights every growing season.

He went to the shed, its green steel roof and dirty white walls covered in scabs of reddish-brown rust, and removed the sea green concrete patio flagstone leaning against the broken door, holding it in place. He had decided long ago that moving and replacing it every time was more convenient than actually repairing the door. And he was not about to change his mind.

Rummaging around inside, he muttered obscenities under his breath and told himself, as he did every spring, that he really needed to take an hour or two and get it organized.

To locate his angle hand-weeder and long-handled pull hoe (four-inch blade), he had to move a broken-down leaf blower, a string-less, gas-powered weed whip, and an electric chainsaw with a burned-out motor. It had been at least ten years since any of these power tools for his yard had been operable. He had no intention of repairing these and several other implements, yet he refused to discard any of them.

His gardening gloves, after fifteen more minutes of crashing, cursing, and banging, were finally discovered in a cupboard with spray paints and varnishes. The cranky old loner, with no friends or family and no visitors in at least three years, was nevertheless convinced somebody had moved them from the shelf he always put them on in late fall after the harvest was finished.

With weeder and hoe in either hand, he left the shed, tripping, inevitably, over the inch-high threshold. The weeds surrounding the cabbage, cauliflower, leeks, and spinach he had planted earlier in the season were attacked with savage determination. After two hours, every unwanted bit of greenery had been annihilated.

All of the chopping and pulling exhausted Tim. Sweat coursed down his face and stung his eyes as he returned the tools to the shed. He was feeling light-headed and didn't notice the numbness creeping along his left arm. When exiting, he again stumbled over the threshold, this time falling to his knees. It took him almost a full minute to struggle to his feet. He forgot to close and prop the shed door with the flagging stone but did notice his old friend John, who had been standing sentinel over the garden for at least twenty years, was in serious need of some new stuffing.

Staggering a bit, he went around the side of the shed and picked up a bale of hay by the binding twine. The grip with his left hand wasn't very good, but he was able to more than compensate with his strong right hand and arm as he carried the bale, stumbling and staggering, over to the scarecrow.

Apologizing first for the impending rough handling, Tim took ol' John off the pine cross, gray with age and starting to split. After carefully laying the tatterdemalion figure on the ground, he stuffed the ragged, faded, hand-me-down overalls and flannel shirt with fistfuls of hay until the scarebird was full and firm in all of its limbs and torso. He carried on his usual one-sided conversation with his silent buddy—chatting about the weather, how much this year's garden would produce and what he planned to do with the bounty and, of course, concerns about depredations by birds, deer, rabbits and those pesky little six-legged critters. More hay replenished its hands (a pair of worn out garden gloves from twenty years ago) and feet (a pair of wool hunting socks with rents in the toes and heels). The head—a used potato sack with eyes, nose, and mouth drawn on in permanent marker—was removed, opened and crammed with more fodder, tied-off and then re-attached with safety pins to the shirt collar. As a final touch, he placed the ancient straw hat— brim frayed and crown with any number of holes—back on its head.

While lifting and hooking the straw man back to its accustomed place on the center post, with his heart clenching like the jaws of a spotted hyena cracking bone for its marrow, he was struck in the chest by a 2,000 gram straight-peen hammer swung with the mighty thews of Beltane the Smith. Crumpling slowly, sucking for oxygen, he was dead by the time he hit the fecund loam of the garden.

⬥

After a week of decomposition and sustenance for two coyotes, what was left of Tim was being picked over by a pair of large, dominant crows who seemed to work in concert. One was savoring the eyeballs while the other feasted on a few scraps of entrails the coyotes overlooked.

These two old friends stayed around for a couple of days finding more bits and pieces of Tim. When not feeding, they were usually perched on either side of the crosspiece of the post on which John was stationed—alone and disconsolate, shoulders slumped and head hanging. Disdaining the (utterly misnamed) scarecrow, they cawed back and forth and drove off any lesser crows who flew by with thoughts of snacking from Tim's remains at the foot of the cross.

The morning was cool and foggy with tendrils of smoky gray lurking along the ground. It had been two weeks since his comrade's death. Time is the surcease of all sorrow. The straw frightener, ever faithful and dutiful, lifted his head and surveyed the garden he had been watching over for more than two decades and found it was plagued with weeds. This would never do. Tim would be so disappointed.

Gathering strength he never knew he had in the stems of his stuffing, the straw being, lugubrious but determined, raised his arms, wrapped them over the crosspiece and lifted off the hook in the back panel of his overalls and lowered himself to the ground.

After a moment of leaning against the post, finding his sea legs, as it were, John knelt down and re-arranged as best he could the clothing put to disarray by the carrion-eaters. In whispery tones like wind through a wheat field, he rattled on about recent weather, how good the squash was doing with no sign of vine borers—oh, but the green peppers were looking poorly from cutworm damage, and early predictions on harvest amounts for the various plantings. During this one-sided discussion, he was taking hay from the bale and stuffing it along the skeletal remains in Tim's tattered shirt and overalls until the limbs and torso were fat and solid. Using twine from the bale, he tied the garden gloves and boots to Tim's frame. As a final touch, he took off his battered straw hat and placed it on Tim's skull.

The old scarecrow lifted the new scarecrow and placed it on the cross. Stalking over to the shed, John retrieved, after some banging around and susurrant cursing, the hoe and weeder. Upon exiting, he stumbled over the shed's threshold. Regaining balance, John closed the door and leaned the green stone against it, then returned to the overgrown garden. Slowly and methodically, he began waging the summer-long war against weeds every gardener fights every growing season.

Ferhoodled on the Island

BARBARA RUTH

Ferhoodle: v. "to confuse, perplex," from Pennsylvania German verhuddle *"to confuse, tangle," related to German* verhudeln *"to bungle, botch." Related: Ferhoodled; ferhoodling.*

We started out as landlopers—that's what brought us to the Island, after all. That and the whispered fables of berries dancing in the rain. I remember when we explored the new world on our recumbent bicycles, regaling one another with recondite treatises on where the berries might be found, what nature of dance they delighted in, when the hell it would rain.

It changed for all of us so slowly, so subtly, that no one caught wind of what becalmed us, only that our explorations were less and less extensive until we only met in the middle, considered our vehicles, but did not mount. Perhaps it was the crepuscular sky, no matter the time of day, which ferhoodled us into this plight: We'd start the day making fine heroic plans and then one of us would make some desultory remark and we'd all be down the rabbit hole. Then there were the discussions. And then the debates, the rants, the coaxings and the credos. We just could not decide. Although the light was soft, the sun had its way with us there in the dappled shadows, and our skins began to turn coriaceous. As our lips cracked, our bare breasts burned.

It. Never. Rained. We called, we sang, in melodies any fruit worthy of the name would surely dance to, "Berries, berries . . . where are you?"

Why didn't they answer us? Some of us wanted to go *mauka*, toward the mountains. Others heard the call of ocean and said we should go *makai*. Still others felt too frangible to move at all. In time we tossed about our our various points of view, our cardinal inclinations as though they were balloons, but in the end the frangibles, the tender ones who wanted to remain among the frangipani, won out. Indecision and lassitude are bosom buddies—that much, I am sure of.

Don't Be Seen

JENNIFER STEPHAN KAPRAL

J.T. unwraps the stained bandages at her wrists, scabs and future scars revealed. She looks at me, her eyes on mine.

I look down. My scales are dull, the bright light of the moon revealing wounds collected from gators, fishhooks, broken glass.

My webbed fingers trace my sharp defects as I clear my throat.

I sing.

1.

The bayou swallowed me when I was still a human, not a child but not yet a teenager. It happened while I was on a walk, trying to momentarily escape the dark thoughts invading my mind, the thoughts that took over when my stepfather's fingers touched my skin, my mother's eyes looked the other way.

Many hours passed. The afternoon heat of Houston stifled my stamina, and the unrelenting sun challenged my desire to be out on my own. Blackness crept into the edges of my vision, my throat cracking with dryness, my skin baking. I slid down the banks of the bayou, untamed grass hitting my skin, bugs biting at my bare legs. Sweat dripped down my armpits, the beads making their way to my hands, hands soon in the water, splashing my arms with relief. Water and skin blended together, my fingers tracing patterns over my cigarette burns.

Hands snaked up from the Bayou, grasping my legs. The hands pulled me down, down into the cloudy water.

I was face-to-face with a creature, something between a woman and a fish. Long black hair floated around her like a net, plastic bottles and beer cans trapped in her tresses. Her thick, scaly tail pulsed with life, sending vibrations through the waters. Her umber skin blended with the murky water surrounding us. It was as if she sprung up from the ground at my toes, born from the mud.

"Do you want to be like me?" she asked, bubbles swirling around us, swells of water stuffing my ears.

I nodded.

"All little girls want to be mermaids. But this isn't a fairy tale."

I snorted, bubbles floating from my mouth to the surface. "I want to be something else. Mermaids aren't human, right? They're fish."

"We're a bit of both. All of the bayou," she said. "You will never have a boyfriend, a husband."

"Do you promise?"

"It's a lonely life. You can't be seen by humans."

"That's what I want."

"You will be ugly."

"I'm already ugly. My nose is too big, my feet too wide. And my skin has marks all over it."

Her eyes scanned me, nostrils flaring as her gaze settled on my scarred arms. She opened her arms wide and chanted, her voice the roar of rain. I swam into her arms, brown water surrounding me in swirls that worked their way through my marked skin, spiraled their way up my too big nose, wrapped themselves inside my wide feet.

2.

Bulky arms push my body up the bayou's concrete banks, my tail leaving a trail of sullied water behind me. Kirby, J.T.'s chihuahua, greets me by licking my skin, skin that matches his fur, matches the mud lingering on the edges of the Bayou.

I pull two fish from my mouth, tossing one to Kirby, the other to J.T. Her pocketknife makes quick work of the fish before tossing it onto her fire. She's hardly recognizable from when I first found her, sucking on discarded chicken bones.

A barrel trashcan lies on its side, providing me with a perfect perch. I slide onto it and sing as I comb my hair with an oversized plastic fork. Today we find three beer cans, a fishhook, a torn t-shirt, several plastic bags, and a flip flop. A crescent moon hangs high above us as we discuss life and make jokes.

"What's uglier than a bayou mermaid?" I ask.

She shrugs her shoulders.

"Yo' mama, of course."

She laughs. "My mom is one ugly bitch. Not so unlike her dyke daughter."

My comb finds a paper receipt, washed blank. "Has anyone messed with you lately?"

She looks at me for a long moment. "No," she says. "No one messes with me anymore."

I toss the blank paper in the trash can beneath me. "I'll tell you another one."

3.

The vastness of the bayous fit me as well as my new fins. My creator leaves in search of bluer waters, giving me the bayou to guard, telling me to follow one rule: Don't be seen.

For years I wear a shield of isolation as I glide through the bayous uninhibited by taxed social workers and cruel classmates. But there are times when my shield cracks, when I am suffocating, water as thick as oil in my lungs, blackness spreading through my blood and pores and brain. I choke as I swim to the surface, craving oxygen I no longer need.

Routine helps bring a calm to my veins, keeping the panic at bay. I set up a daily swim along my favorite tributary at the end of the night, before the trails fill with joggers and bikers and strollers. I savor the last minutes of dark before bearing down deep, sheltered from the sun and people, running my hands along the smooth floor, collecting treasures to leave for fishermen and the homeless.

The same woman is always the first runner to appear, my signal to fade away. She has short legs and wears the same pink hat every morning. She runs through rain and humidity and swarms of mosquitoes. She dodges piles of trash that accumulate after the bayou swells with rain then shrinks with the sun. She never sees me, her focus straight ahead, never off course.

The banks are high. It rained all night, so I'm close to the trails. She doesn't see the man approach, and I don't either—until it's too late. He has her on the ground, she's hitting and biting and screaming. He has a knife and a look of destruction in his eyes, a familiar look that turns my boiling bayou blood cold. He hits her across the face and reaches for her shorts.

His ankle is a small branch in my hand. I snap it. He cries out, swears, slaps the woman. My tail strikes his face hard once, then twice, blood squirting from his nose and ears before he loses consciousness. I swish him into the water in one swift swoop.

The woman stares at me. I hold my breath, fins flapping. She stands up, wipes the blood from her face.

"I guess I should stop running at dark," she says.

"I don't think so," I say, my unused voice raw.

She eyes me, hands shaking. She snorts, blood and snot coming from her nose. I laugh, the warrior laugh of a siren, the call of a victor. She eyes me again and then laughs, tears flowing from her face, mixing with blood and snot. Her feet move, she's running, small drops of blood trailing behind her. I swim next to her, deep beneath the surface, leaving the attacker behind with the other lost but not missed items at the bottom of the bayou.

The next morning, she returns. She scans the water for me. I surface briefly before diving behind my brown shield. I have broken the one rule, cracking it in half like a crawfish and sucking out the middle, devouring a moment gone too quickly, leaving me looking for the next bite.

4.

"What else?" J.T. asks. She pushes up the sleeves of her oversized hoodie, baggy clothes hiding feminine curves.

I weave together the lowest notes I can find.

Screams, so loud I hear them from the floor of the bayou. I swim to the peak of the surface, my hair spreading wide and hiding me.

A toddler stands at the bank of the bayou, reaching a chubby arm towards the water with curiosity. The mother is running down the concrete bank, but she will be too late. The toddler is in my waters, chubby legs and arms kicking furiously as it sinks to the bottom.

In seconds the toddler is in my arms. A deep longing feels me, vibrating through my barren middle, singing through blood and lungs and fins. I could make the child mine, joining me in these waters. It would be cared for, never neglected for a second.

I start my chanting but stop almost immediately, surfacing just as the mother is about to throw herself into the bayou. The desperation in her eyes matches mine, maternal instinct driving us to the unthinkable.

The toddler chokes in my arms, water dripping from her pink dress. My fingers pinch her small nose and I breath into her lungs, my life force filling her body. I pull away and she gapes at me, her chunky arms and legs still, her mouth open in awe. She will forever carry a piece of the bayou with her, longing to be in the waters everyone else finds hideous.

My eyes are locked on my almost-child as I swim to the shore. I hand her to her mother, who lets out a loud sob that still rings in my ears. She grips the child tight, brown water mixing with salty tears.

I speed headlong back into the current, resurfacing minutes later, feeling the desperation for oxygen. The mother and child are gone. I let the rocking chair rhythm of the water rush through my body, salt burning my throat, salt running down my face.

5.

J.T. is gone. Her usual spot under I-45 is filled with water. She packed her shopping cart and headed to higher ground at my warning, leaving me to work.

I sing as the rain pommels the concrete, pushing most people away.

For those who cannot ignore the Siren call of home, I dive into submerged cars. For those who are heartbroken, I hunt for lost animals. For those who are called to help man, I propel kayaks forward from underneath their bellies. I am lost to human sight, the frenzy of life shining bright and blocking out a woman of the mud.

A snake slides through my fingers, its olive green diamonds swirling in front of me. The fury of rapidly-rising waters bound the snake to the tree, a plastic grocery bag choking it. I pull the bag and the snake breaks free, slinking into the water, but I am now surrounded by mud. I flop my tail to try to move towards the bayou, but only slide further away. The sun is due to rise. My heart beats faster, breathing becoming labored as my fins long for water.

A group abandons their kayaks, gathers near the edge of the water. Rain pounds on their neon shirts, already stained from bayou muck. Lights flash from their helmets, focusing on my widening eyes. I freeze, hoping they think they are imagining something, between the rain and the darkness. But they inch closer until they are just a few feet away.

I sit up, pushing back one last desperate time, getting nowhere.

One steps forward. "We've heard about you. Do you need help?"

A clump of mud falls off my arm, running down my body in rivers. "You've heard of me?"

"They call you the mother of the bayou," one says.

My heart is in my throat. "I can't be seen, they'll hunt me and—"

"May we help you?"

The sun is rising fast. Desperation fuels my nod as I grind my sharp molars, tense my fins.

They surround me, pick me up on all sides. Their fingers are gentle, grip strong as they set me back in my homewaters.

I spear into the bayou before tumbling back, resurfacing at a safe distance. The humans are no longer visible through the roar of the rain, the current a pulse hammering through the center of Houston.

Urban Coyotes at the Hyatt

TY PHELPS

The urban coyotes have gathered at a conference. They've come from Nashville, Minneapolis, Portland, Santa Fe. The topic is whether remaining subtropical floral ecosystems could support micro-marketing revenue generation. Targets to hit, quotas to meet. Resources must not go untapped. The conference is less sparsely attended than the conference organizers, a committee of business people and professors of biology, anticipated. Large crowds of creatures hum through the hotel consulting programs on their phones. The organizers puff their chests as they move through the hotel lobby with their special sky-blue lanyards.

This year there are seven coyotes in attendance. Three of them have souls of past human executives stuck deep inside them, below the larynx. Burt's Bees, HP, Old Spice. Former souls of the other coyotes are buried too deep within themselves to be deciphered.

In the crowded Hyatt bar, the coyotes linger in a booth in the back corner. People drink and chatter. It's dimly lit. The booth is a soft maroon. There are people curled on the barstools, and an old porcupine chewing the straw in his empty tumbler. The coyotes lap whisky out of ashtrays and laugh when the bartender shatters a wineglass. Later, they'll get moon-howling drunk and make investments on the internet. Some will have nightmares of the desert at night, when it's cold and bare, the moonlight falling like snow. The eyes of their relatives hover over the landscape, their faces lonely and sad.

The coyotes are all Hyatt Gold members. They hear the perks of membership ping in their inboxes. They count the points they accrue and try not to think about the desert, or how ominous everything is, deep under the hotel lights.

There's a pool on the 35th floor, and an exercise room with a sauna. They splash in the pool and laugh at each other when the chlorine mousses their fur into spikes. In the evening, they order each other too-early wake-up calls and excessive room service. One of the coyotes doesn't have an expense account, and pleads to be left out of the pranks. The others cite Darwin and ignore him. He slinks away to his room.

Some sleep on the floor. Others climb under the over-tucked sheets and sink into the mattresses, and dream dreams that float between two separate worlds.

The keynote speaker this year is a lecturer at an undergraduate program specializing in business administration. As a student, she studied biology and art history. The glow of the projected PowerPoint creates a long shadow. Her hands claw the podium. She's discovered a tension in her shoulders that she feels symbolizes the fluctuating truths of her profession. She tries to reconcile humanity's dependence on nature with its dominion over it. She has begun to have night sweats and dreams about the desert. The adolescent philosophical equilibrium she established with her undergraduate thesis stubbornly refuses to be restored.

The coyotes sense in her a reflection of their own circumstances. They can sense, dimly, a coyote peeking out from behind her human eyelids, and after her talk they invite her to play Big Buck Hunter in the hotel bar and to talk about the dignity of the hunt and the necessity of scavenging. She accepts and they get moon-howling drunk together and debate whether the world is more wonderful than it used to be.

The next day at breakfast, the coyotes gather at their table in the biggest conference room. Many tables are full of ruminants, relaxing in their tailored suits. One of the coyotes tells the others about a time in which he and a trio of elk started a social group under a streetlight in a suburb outside Chicago, and how they ate from the little oases of grass that grew out of cracks in the concrete and composed mental letters to their friends back in the mountains. He tells of how an old woman joined them, tentatively at first, hovering just outside the pool of light, but gradually she grew bolder. Finally, she defied her husband, who spied behind their screen door. She brought them all baked goods and made suggestions for naming the group, and she even chased off the neighborhood association when they trooped up with their clipboards to complain about zoning violations.

The other coyotes wet napkins and wipe the maple syrup that sticks to the fur around their mouths. They listen and nod. None of them know what the others are thinking.

Dreaming of the Chaos

DOROTHY TINKER

I keep dreaming of the Chaos. It haunts my sleep and my waking hours alike. It sends me into a cold sweat and makes my heart race as hope and disappointment war against each other within my mind to the point of mingling into a single emotion.

Last night, my dreams were filled with racing creatures, myself among them. We ran and ran until the end of the course. I was so close to the front of the pack that I could taste victory. Then something shifted. I don't know if it was me, the creatures, or simply the dream, but that victory was stolen from my grasp with a speed and utter apathy that left a bitter taste in my mouth.

The night before that I dreamed of stolen love. My mind was filled with beings who treated me with utter respect and the utmost decency. They offered me sanctuary for my secrets and a safe harbor during my times of weakness. Then, when I was certain of my love, they attacked me using the very knowledge of secrets and weaknesses I had given them, destroying my reputation and my life.

They say it is better to have loved and lost than to have never loved at all, but that dream made me doubt that such a phrase held truth.

I keep dreaming of the Chaos. Hope and Fear, Love and Hate have already flooded my dreams. Tonight, I know I will dream of War and Peace, but I do not fear whatever dream might come with them. Nay, I do not fear tonight for I know I will wake in the morning. Yet tomorrow night . . .

Do I dare sleep tomorrow night when I know the Chaos that Life and Death were born to face will visit my mind?

Do I dare sleep when I know I might never awaken, and yet never die?

The Way of Things

BONNIE JO STUFFLEBEAM

I wake to find that my hand has turned to steel. The arm stings where the metal meets flesh at the wrist, silver fading into gray like dead flesh, then coloring back into the shade of my skin. My wife sleeps beside me. I do not wake her.

To lift the hand is a chore. My wrist throbs as I pull it to my chest and hold it there like the child I've sworn I'll never have. Not with my genes. Not with my father's liquid curse lurking in the cells of the arm I cradle. At least the still human bits. I don't know where the steel came from or if it has cells that carry the past. But it feels right, that my hand should be this way. I gaze at the silver reflection of my twisted face. Some mornings, I do not recognize myself. In the steel, distorted, I am clear as the light outside the window blinds. I hope that the metal does not leave. I wish that the metal had come sooner. I wonder if it would have changed things.

My father's memory has been funneled through the fist-shaped hole he punched in the wall outside my childhood bedroom. He was trying, he said, to turn out the light. But when he came in every night to tuck the covers around me, he reeked of vodka. I never questioned the smell. It was the way of things.

I was eight and did not know better.

I was ten and wished I had the strength to take him out myself.

I was twelve, crouching at the foot of the stairs, listening to a wife's empty threats. If he didn't stop, she would leave him.

I was twenty, and he was a glinting blaze in the middle of a field. Too drunk to drive. Pulled into a nearby farm. Fell asleep with a cigarette in his mouth. I was twenty with a phone clutched to my ear. They said the words: "Your father is dead." And I felt nothing.

Would his son's metal hand have scared him sober? At least I could have closed it around his throat until he stopped yelling. There was an anger then that made me shake in bed at night. Now there is nothing. An empty feeling, like I haven't eaten in years.

When my wife, Jillian, sees the hand, she holds her hands over her open mouth.

"What did you do to yourself?" she says. "Have you called the doctor?"

I am eating toast with blackberry jam. It tastes like bread and fruit and leaves a sticky feeling on my flesh hand. The steel feels nothing.

"No need," I say.

"No need?" She grabs at the counter, as though she is about to fall over. In the dark of our kitchen, for I have not yet turned on the lights, she is a shadowy face and the silhouette of worry. It must hurt to worry so much. Inside her chest there must be pain like constant heartburn. When we met in college, it was nice to have someone to worry about me. These days it's just as it is; there is no nice or not nice. The bread tastes like bread. I take another bite.

"I like it this way," I say. "It feels like it should have always been this way."

For a moment we are both silent. "I'm going out," she says. It's been months since we spent a morning together at the breakfast table, spreading jam on bread, like we used to. I think she got tired of the silence. I am okay with her leaving, if it means I do not have to pretend to care about the day's news or the day's plans. I watch her go. At the door, she flips on the light. Then she is gone. I flex my fingers. They are the most beautiful things I have ever seen.

The next morning, when I wake, both my arms are steel. Three toes. A patch of skin around my navel is greying. I touch the spot with my metal fingers, and the surfaces clink together like a new music. The morning after that, my legs and feet are steel. They crash across the kitchen floor.

"Do something," Jillian says. "Please, John, just do something." She waits with her hand on the front doorknob.

"What can I do?" I ask.

She says nothing. She stares across the room, eyes wide and wanting. What can I do?

Soon I am all metal outside, though inside I still feel my heart beating. When I dream of my father, I do not wake with gasping breaths. When my wife leaves the house without explanation, I do not wonder who the other man is, though the thought of his hands used to fill me with a great hot rage. I do not go to work. I sit at the kitchen table and crush apples in my palms. Their gore is red and messy and human.

When my wife returns and slides into our bed, I try to touch her so that I will know how it feels to touch skin with steel. She rolls away from me.

"What is wrong?" I say.

"I can't," she says. "Not while you're like that. Change back. Please."

"I don't know how," I say, but that is not all of the truth. I can't change back because I am myself now more than I ever was before. I am everything I ever wanted to be.

Jillian and I were happy once. Once there was breakfast in bed and late nights laughing and homemade chicken soup when we were sick. Once there was her singing in the shower and dances she did with her fingers across my stomach and the sound of her typing in the next room. Now there is an empty house, and no drive behind her eyes.

I was thirty-eight, and a father was resurrected in a fist. I hit the wall. The plaster caved around me. My knuckles bled. I shut myself down. There was no other way to keep us safe.

I was thirty-nine. I could no longer tell her that I loved her. I no longer did. There was no love left.

The heart slows. The stomach does not growl. I open my mouth each morning and no breath comes out. I am solid. I am heavy. I am smooth and cold and perfect. There is no more dull morning sun; it is a prism of lights now that reaches through our bedroom window. Because the light is part of another world, because no one but me sees it, I do not belong beside a wife who sleeps when the sun is beaming bright. I wait at the breakfast table for her to wake. I want to know all of the world.

Jillian stopped asking me to change. She stopped turning on the light. The morning of my solidness, as she comes down the stairs, I know that that there is something to her now that there never was before. She sits across from me. She eats an apple. She wipes the juice away with the back of her hand.

"I guess I can no longer pretend that you're someone else," she says. "That you're warm inside, that you care about something, anything. I guess I can't pretend that you're someone you're not anymore."

"Yes," I say. "You are correct."

"I knew when I married you that you were hardened. But I couldn't help it." She cries, and the tears run with the juice and drip on the table. "I felt safe around you. You loved me in your cold way, and it didn't scare me like other love did. I wasn't ready to be loved the way another man could love me."

"Yes," I say. "You often smelled of him, when you crept into bed at night. I cannot smell it any longer. It is good."

She turns her face and hides her eyes behind her hand. "Don't you feel anything anymore? Don't you love me? Aren't you angry? You used to get so angry. And it was terrible, but at least it was something. I could run from anger. I can't run from nothing." She looks as though she is trying to shrink herself down. I want to tell her that it is impossible. That there is nowhere for her mass to go. But it would do no good to tell her this. She knows. The apple core sits naked on the table, now.

"You speak like one of flesh and blood," I say. "I cannot speak like that anymore. I do not know what anger is. But I should like to see if it still sleeps inside me. Take me to him. I want to wish you a fair goodbye."

My father hated other men. Once he attacked the next door neighbor for helping my mother bring the groceries in.

He used to call when he was at work to make sure that she was home. I used to dream of other men. I dreamt of them running their hands over Jillian's thighs, kissing the fuzz between her legs, undressing her at the window as I watched. I no longer dream. I used to wake with sweat beaded on my forehead. I no longer sweat. I used to feel the urge to pull Jillian to my chest and squeeze her as tight as I could. There are worse emotions than anger.

"Remember," she says, as we drive down twisted roads in neighborhoods I have never seen, "when we used to drive, just anywhere we could? I would tell you to take me somewhere beautiful?" She grips the wheel. "What happened to us?"

Once I took her to a river where my friends and I used to down whole bottles of vodka. Another time I took her to a rundown park where there were no more children. The last time we drove, I took her to the field where my father burned alive.

"I remember," I say.

"We don't have to do this," she says. "We can just leave it alone. I'll go my way. You can go yours. We tried."

We drive past houses with for sale signs outside, past a kid's tricycle left in a yard. We come to a red brick apartment building. She parks the car. She looks at me for a moment. The seat is broken under my weight. When I open the door to climb out, I crack the handle in half. She opens my door from the outside. We walk together up a stone path to a red door. She knocks.

"Are you sure?" she says.

The door opens. The man is brittle thin and familiar, though I do not think we have met.

"He asked to see you," Jillian says. The man holds his arms out to his sides. He is shaking. Jillian, too. Her hands are pressed together so hard they are white.

"Here I am," says the man. "See?"

"May we come in?" I ask. I do not wait for him to answer. I shove past him. His apartment is full of things. I stand while Jillian and the man she addresses as Michael whisper at the door. I hear what they say. He is angry, but it is not my anger. It is a brittle anger, full of cracks and holes.

I do not think that my anger lives anymore. To be sure, I step close and push them together.

"Kiss," I say.

They hesitate. I push them again. They kiss closed-mouthed.

"Again," I say. They linger.

"One more time," I say.

They latch. Her arms wrap around his neck. They are both trembling of fear and glee. I watch with eyes unclouded by love. It is something, this coupling, that I have never known, not even when I was skin. They fit, the brittle man and the broken woman

It is good that they should have this.

I leave the apartment. I walk. Somewhere, maybe there is this for ones like me, too. Maybe there are others of metal. Maybe I will find them. Or maybe I will wake one morning and be skin again. I walk. Whatever happens, it will be the way of things. Each step I take booms like a heartbeat.

Darker Ages Yet

JOHN DUTTERER

Every air conditioner in the city was set on ten, screaming air that was cool but not cold anymore, and the window units incontinently dripped gray water onto the sidewalks. Blinds down, we sat on our hairy couches watching TV weather reports, which were repetitive, to say the least.

Somewhere, the generators coughed and then shuddered. We dreaded an outage, yet expected it.

Barely evening, darkness overflowed its bounds. Absence of light was followed by silence, a sound almost peaceful, were it not for its awkward ramifications. Gasps, groans, and curses erupted. A few laughs were also heard, but in the entire city, only a few. Soon the muscular heat pried at the windows, crawling under doors.

We couldn't help being spooked as if a vast hand closed over us. The air grew fat with carbon dioxide, and we moved slower and slower, our bodies having perhaps their own reliance upon electrical power.

My 14-year-old son came in from outside, and rather than alluding to the blackout or the heat, he simply said, "I'm surprised by all the goats out there. And I saw people on horses."

Questioning him uncovered no further information. After finding our flashlights, he and I went outside and it was just as he said, the streets had become barnyards. A lamb stood on our front doorstep, panting. We could easily judge the completeness of the power outage as the first stars of evening appeared, unchallenged by neon. No cars were to be seen on our street, nor any heard from afar. Silence returned, falling like rain, disrupted at times by the sound of hooves scraping on concrete. At some other distance, there was a clang of metal and human shouts, expressing either surprise or desperation.

"I think they sound angry," my son said.

We went back inside, fearing rioters. My wife lit a candle and was now playing some sort of primitive harpsichord. Seriously, the harpsichord? The interior of our house felt cooler after being outside, but the air was rank with the smell of unfamiliar meat.

When I asked what it was, my adult daughter replied, "We have no idea." She turned her attention back to her loom, spinning by the light of a torch. A torch? Since when did we have one of those wall sockets—braziers? And it held a burning bundle of kindling. I wanted to say something, but was even more concerned by the smell from the kitchen. An unfamiliar old woman was stirring a pot on our stove, which was itself nothing more than an open flame. I asked who she was, and with a toothless smile she answered, "Why, 'tis Gavelda, m'lord."

Startled, I waded backward through the darkness to find my wife and ask how and when this intruder entered.

"She is one of our vassals, I think."

Ready as I was to respond, "Ah. Of course," I could not. We have never had employees or servants. "She needs to leave."

"She probably lives here, in one of these rooms." My wife looked up into the interior void of our home, which was almost completely unfamiliar, the issue of poor visibility aside. The ceilings felt high, based on the echoes of our voices, and the hallways likewise stretched too far into the invisible distance.

Determined to personally evict the cook, I turned and then turned again. I could no longer find the kitchen. Something hairy brushed my leg, darting off down the hall.

"The dog," a voice said.

I shined my light on a gaunt man with a reddish beard. "But you are?"

"'Tis I, Reynaldo."

"Reynaldo?"

"Your seneschal, sire."

Petulantly slapping my thighs, I cried out, "Get out of here! Get that dog out of here! And the cook!"

After an awkward pause, "As you wish, sire."

I found my way to a chair, an uncomfortable wooden one. Soon Reynaldo unfastened the heavy bolts of our front door with one hand, holding the spaniel by the scruff with the other. His effort was extreme, but the massive door slowly swung open. No light entered from outside, only the clang of battle. The determined servant thrust the dog out and slammed the door on its paw. After meticulously sealing the door again, Reynaldo disappeared, only to return with the cook. She struggled at first but then submitted meekly and stood by while my henchman unlocked the vault-like enclosure once more. I have no idea where my quadruple-locked door even came from.

My son appeared at my side, holding his torch aloft and verifying that I was the right person. "Father, it's too late for Mother." When had he ever called me anything other than "Dad"?

"Then she should go to bed."

His voice caught in his throat. He looked equally inclined to laugh or to scream. "'Twould seem she is fallen with the plague." Sobs bubbled out of him.

"Come on now. No one dies of the plague anymore, except maybe in some place like India."

"Where's that?"

"Never mind. Let's go see her, and we can call an ambulance."

"Call a—?"

He led me to a rather remote room where my wife was, in fact, on the brink of death. A gnarled man in a filthy smock was in the process of bleeding her with a blade, and when I entered he said, "You'll be lucky if your whole clan hasn't already come down with the death, my lord. I speak plainly, so you will know I am in earnest. You must isolate yourselves."

"Get out of here!" I grabbed him where a collar should have been, and as I pushed him toward the door, he stumbled. My son sank down, burying his face in his mother's pillow. I struck him with my gloved hand (who wears gloves indoors in the summer?) and said, "Fool! Go on, take the disease upon thyself and die in turn." I had never hit him or spoken thus to him, and yet it felt appropriate. "Many have died, and more yet shall travel that way. Even she that bore you has gone, and we cannot know what the morrow brings." He looked at me incredulously, either from disagreement or because my speech patterns were changing along with my conduct.

As I left the room I nearly collided with a procession of priests and monks who were, no doubt, coming to offer my wife a Christian burial. They were all dressed in immaculate vestments, each of stoic comportment, and though their eyes were lively with grief, their skin was chalk white. Only one spoke, intoning some solemn prayer that asks for mercy but begs for judgment.

As I groped my way down the hall, cursing the servants for not preparing more torches, I heard horrible little claws scratching along the flagstones. We should have retained that dog as an antidote for vermin. Hissing flames were all that kept us from rats omnipresent and night without end.

My daughter was slumped over her loom when I found her. I wanted to help, to touch her, but I knew better. Her essence was gone. I slumped back down into the uncomfortable chair and attempted to weep. When my son saw his sister, he threw himself on the ground.

Reynaldo returned, looking ghoulish by torchlight. "He has the sickness, my lord. Put him outside and have no regret."

I weighed this possibility, trying to think clearly, but felt ready to fall over. "I am not well myself . . . Reynaldo."

A look of genuine fear was upon him, knowing as he must how utterly the plague afflicted this house.

House? Chateau. Fortress.

The lights came back on with guillotine suddenness, bringing a wave of electronic noise that left us staggered. There we stood half-blinded, half-dead amid decaying finery in this futuristic world, each of us trying to discover a difference from the darker place we had known.

Phantasmal

PAUL STANSBURY

The foolish believe the phantasmal can trouble the living. Not true. We have no more substance than the vagaries of dreams and nightmares that linger in the mind upon waking. An uneasy feeling that evaporates like the steam of morning coffee. No, it is the machinations of the living that pose the threat. Not that we are not without desire to bend the future to our designs, we merely lack the impetus. While we may possess the psychic vigor, we miss the physical impulse. Consequently, we are quite unable to do much more than wander about, yearning for the corporal comfort we have lost through the death of flesh. This is, of course, a misfortunate existence.

My dearest wife and I were shot for three dollars and our mule. We were in our cabin above Deer Run Creek. I was in the main room of our cabin when the raiders, murderous thugs masquerading as soldiers, burst through the door, pistols drawn. A single gunshot ripped through my gut. Hearing the noise, Rufina rushed in from the kitchen only to catch a bullet straight through her chest. She was dead before she slumped to the floor. Lying next to her, I lingered all afternoon and into the night. Our murderers bore no anxiety of conscience caused by regret for doing wrong or causing pain. They left us to die without contrition or remorse, angered only by the pittance of their murderous gains. They were not alone in their anger.

There is an old house standing on the foundation of our cabin. It is the finer of the two built there over these many years. I can only wonder what Chad thought when Melissa pushed the ladder out from under his feet. He asked her to steady it while he climbed to the top rungs, two stories up, to clear ice from the sagging gutter. He instinctively grasped the rotting metal as the ladder pitched to the side. Did he realize in the instant before the rusted nails gave way what she had done?

I think he would have thought it impossible. After all, it was he who had pulled her body from the icy water. They had been ice skating on the creek when she had fallen through. We had seen Melissa's phantasmal roiling away in confusion, purged from its corporeal home. All the while, he knelt beside the lifeless body, forcing his breath into its lungs.

There are those rare interregnums between life and death. Pauses, if you will, between the last breath and the irrevocable corruption of the flesh. Divergences from the instantaneous, indeterminable periods, during which a phantasmal, purged from its corporeal limits, can return. For most, the moment passes before they realize their opportunity. In that case, death wins out. Sometimes, however, a phantasmal returns, and life is resumed. The living have a habit of calling that a miracle. That is what Chad called it when her chest heaved and she began to breathe again.

His body lies there on the frozen ground. She kneels beside him, pressing her hands over his nose and mouth until he is still. I see his phantasmal welling up, shapeless, roiling in the confusion that always comes with the fracture of the temporal bond. There is no guarantee the body will be serviceable after such trauma, but try I must. As the last vestige of his phantasmal leaves, I enter. What exquisite pain! My throat shudders open and my lungs suck down a ragged breath. Warm, soft lips kiss my brow. It will take some time to heal, but I know I will make it with dear Rufina at my side.

As I said, no phantasmal can trouble the living. No, it is the machinations of the living that pose the threat.

We Are the Cost

L.C. LARA

We were the sentries.

We protected the deep woods and were her first line of defense. We thrived at life with her inhabitants, living in complete symbiosis.

My brothers and I held weary birds aloft on our limbs and sheltered skittish mice below ground. The squirrels and the deer helped deliver our seed to fresh ground and founded new groves.

A small black bear once made its home in a brush pile at our feet. We watched the young female bear nose and paw our fallen leaves into a pile. She dug her claws into our flesh, shredding and tearing the bark from our trunks. Stinging wounds that turned into scars. We stood tall and alive through the pain. We breathed for the bears and the bears breathed for us. Symbiotic.

Over time, men arrived with their weapons and one by one, in waves, we fell. Mockingbirds mimicked the high pitched thrum of the saws as the deep woods receded, forced to the point of implosion, giving way to progress. Birds moved tree to tree, further toward the center of what was once a far reaching forest.

How much must we lose?

The young mother bear beneath my canopy birthed a set of cubs, a boy and a girl. I dropped dry needles to form a pillow for the mother and a burrow for the cubs. The mother scavenged for food, never finding enough for three starving bears. We stood watch as the cubs grew, one faster than the other, and we felt the sky's cold tears when the smallest cub died. In the end his flesh provided nourishment for his mother and sister.

Day after day more men came, and day after day more of my fellow sentries fell to their saws, cut down at the knee. Their joints vibrated with each swing of their axes. They were hacked, beaten, and shattered until finally delivered to death. Our protective forces dwindled, leaving the deep woods vulnerable. They killed us and used our bodies as the skeletons in their houses and as the protective shields around their yards.

It wouldn't be much longer until their destructive path reached me. The animals knew it, the ground knew it. The family of hawks in a neighboring tree abandoned its nest. A young fledgling failed to find her wings and fell to her death. No one noticed but the young cub hiding at my feet.

The mother bear fell asleep last week. Her cub nuzzled into her thick black fur when she heard the echoes and felt the tremors under her paws as my brothers' bodies crashed against the earth. The cub braved the few steps from her mother's body to the next tree, encouraged by hunger, to retrieve the baby bird. She dropped the dead hawk in front of her mother's dry nose as an offering. An offering her mother did not accept. The cub eventually ingested the feathers and bones herself.

Then my cub disappeared. My birds were long gone. The mice and squirrels had found shelter elsewhere.

And the men finally found their way to me. They chopped me down, piled my discarded broken pieces at the edge of the dying forest and set me on fire. In front of me stood the manmade houses. Behind me stood what was left of the nature-grown structures. And I lay in the middle: charred, empty, destroyed.

An arid wind whipped over me, sparks and ash catching a ride on its current. The fire meant only for me spread, rippling to engulf everything around me.

The men released a predator they could not control. The earth was burning, taking back what was stolen. Rows and rows of houses were smothered behind smoke clouds as dark as charcoal. Orange flaming fingers flicked through breaks in the smog. Caught between, my brothers and me. We were the seam.

And we are the cost of progress.

CONTRIBUTORS

John Dutterer's prose most recently appears in *Unlikely Stories* and the April 2016 edition of *Right Hand Pointing*, while his numerous poetry publications include *False Cosmopolitan,* an e-chapbook by *White Knuckle Press.* An employee in the book and music industry, John retires each evening to Glen Burnie, an ancient suburb of Baltimore.

Paul Hostovsky is the author of eight books of poetry, most recently *The Bad Guys,* which won the FutureCycle Poetry Book Prize for 2015. His work has appeared in many journals and anthologies, including *Carolina Quarterly, Poetry East, Shenandoah, The Sun, Bellvue Literary Review, Natural Bridge, Poet Lore* and others. He has won a Pushcart Prize, two Best of the Net Awards, the Muriel Craft Bailey Award from the *Comstock Review,* and has been featured on Poetry Daily, Verse Daily, and The Writer's Almanac. His ninth book of poems, *Is That What That Is,* is forthcoming from FutureCycle Press in 2017. He makes his living in Boston as an ASL interpreter. To read more of his work, visit him at paulhostovsky.com.

Jennifer Stephan Kapral writes poetry, nonfiction, and fiction. She was born in the shadows of steel mills in Western PA and studied creative nonfiction at the University of Pittsburgh. She currently resides in Houston, TX, spending time by the bayous with her husband and two dogs.

L.C. Lara is currently working toward her master's degree in creative writing with the University of Denver. More of her writing can be found in *Crack the Spine Literary Magazine.* She is a wife, mother, and former school teacher turned dance teacher. When she's not busy family-ing, reading, writing, or dancing, she likes volunteering her time with Writespace. She's lived south, north, west, and now east of Houston; no matter how many times she moves she's never very far from the city.

Sylvia J. Martínez is a writer, adult school ESL teacher, and private tutor. Her work has appeared in *The East Bay Review, Cipactli, Word Riot, Tattoo Highway*, and *The San Francisco Examiner*, among others. She earned her M.F.A. from San Francisco State and is working on her first collection of stories. She lives in the S.F. Bay Area with her husband, two teenage children, and dog.

From blog superhero for a spec fiction mag to journalist for a high-end coffee table publication, multi-genre writer **Jody T. Morse** likes to play the field when it comes to writing. Her ability to produce quality written work about a vast array of topics has sent her career down many 'paths less traveled'. While technical writing isn't out of the question, enrapturing readers through emotional prose is where Jody finds her most prolific sense of joy. Currently, she has three books in various stages of process: *Finding Yoshiko*, a YA novella about abandonment, adoption and the true definition of family; *One in Paris, One in Prison*, a memoir that she's co-authoring with her baby sister; and *Feathers of the Phoenix*, a fantasy romp through the life of Lady Divinia of Lancaster that is part historical fiction, part romance and part mystical adventure. After all of that, are you ready for the name drop dump? Just to list a few to wet your whistle: *ArtHouston magazine, Luna Station Quarterly, Texas Living Magazine*, and *Verbatim Poetry*. This writer of humor, sophistication and love is a member of the Writespace Writing Center, Northwoods Writers Guild and Woodlands Writers Guild—anthology pieces have been or are being published. Winner of the May 2016, WILDsound Festival's One-Page Story Contest, Jody has also contributed to quite a few corporate websites and done some ghostwriting. When not feverishly typing away on her own pieces, Jody contributes to the Writership editing collective, as an assistant to the Executive Editor. Living on an 18-acre farmstead in the heart of a national forest, Jody has plenty to inspire her creative juices and many hammocks to choose from when reading rather than writing. See pics of Jody's hideaway home and learn even more about her, yes there is more, at www.bountifulbalconybooks.com.

Eloísa Pérez-Lozano grew up bilingual and bicultural in Houston, Texas. She graduated from Iowa State University with her M.S. in journalism and mass communication and her B.S. in psychology. She is a long-distance member of the Latino Writers Collective in Kansas City, and a member of the Gulf Coast Poets and The Poetry Society of Texas. Her poetry has been featured in *The Texas Observer, aaduna, Diverse Voices Quarterly, The Acentos Review,* and VONA's Voices against Racial Injustice: An Arts Forum, among others.

M. Kelly Peach is a long-time bureaucrat with the State of Michigan and a father of four and grandfather of two (soon to be three). He enjoys hunting, camping, fishing, and is a bibliophile who loves to collect and read books. He has been published in diverse markets such as: *Punchkin's, Alternate Hilarities I-III, Mad Scientist Journal* (Summer 2014), *The Graveyard* (anthology), *Woods-N-Water News, Unsung Stories,* and *Cheapjack Pulp.* You can see more about him at peachmme.tumblr.com.

Ty Phelps is a writer of short fiction and poetry. He teaches middle and high school English and private percussion lessons in Portland, OR, where he lives with his wife and their cat. He holds a BA in Literature from Carleton College and a Masters of Teaching English from Lewis and Clark College. He is the winner of *The Gravity of the Thing*'s 2016 Six Word Story Contest.

Barbara Ruth is a photographer, poet, fiction writer, essayist and memoirist living in San Jose, CA. Her work is widely anthologized in feminist, queer, literary and disability collections. She was San Diego Area Coordinator of California Poets in the Schools and a recipient of a California Arts Council Artist In Residence Grant at the San Diego Jewish Community Center. She has performed her writing with Mothertongue Readers Theater, Wry Crips Disabled Women's Theater Group and the Jewish Lesbian Writers Group, all in the San Francisco Bay Area, Her work appears in publications based in Canada, Australia, the UK and the US.

Jyotsna Sreenivasan's novel *And Laughter Fell From the Sky* was published in 2012 by HarperCollins. Her short fiction has appeared in numerous literary magazines and anthologies. She received an Artist Fellowship Grant from the Washington, DC Commission on the Arts. She currently work as a secondary school teacher in Columbus, Ohio. For more information, please see her website: SecondGenStories.com

Paul Stansbury is a lifelong native of Kentucky. Now retired, he lives in Danville, Kentucky. His stories have appeared in the anthologies, *Brief Grislys*, published by Apocryphile Press, *Neo-Legends To Last A Deathtime* published by KY Story, *Frightening* published by SEZ Publishing, and *Out of the Cave* published by MacKenzie Publishing. His work has also appeared in a variety of online publications. His poetry has appeared in *The Rising Phoenix Review*, *Young Ravens Literary Review* and *Kentucky Monthly*. He is a guest writer for the *Danville Advocate Messenger Newspaper*. He frequently reads his work in public. He is also the Scheduling Coordinator for Historic Penn's Store Annual Kentucky Writers Celebration.

Bonnie Jo Stufflebeam's fiction has appeared in magazines such as *Clarkesworld*, *The Toast*, *Lightspeed*, and *Beneath Ceaseless Skies*. She lives in Texas with her partner and two literarily-named cats: Gimli and Don Quixote. She holds an MFA in Creative Writing from the University of Southern Maine's Stonecoast program and curates the annual Art & Words Show. You can visit her on Twitter @BonnieJoStuffle or through her website: www.bonniejostufflebeam.com.

Dorothy Tinker is a writer of epic fantasy novels and short stories that run the gamut from scifi/fantasy/spiritual to horror to romance/erotica. She is the author of the young adult epic fantasy series, *Peace of Evon*, which also includes *Gift of War* and *Lost King*. With a fascination for languages and cultures, she incorporates both other languages and other cultures into the works that she writes.

Alexis Vaughan is a mother, artist and business founder. After a decade as a professional actor, she recently took a break to start a family, and found that her creative energies turned toward writing. Alexis writes mainly poetry and poetic narrative, and is a member of Write on Mamas. More information: @mymyvaughan and mymyvaughan.com.

Christopher Walker is a writer and English teacher based in Bielsko-Biala in the South of Poland. He is the author of the book for children, *The Man in the Mango Tree*. He is married and has two children, Zuzanna and Matylda. Find him online at www.closelyobserved.com.

ACKNOWLEDGMENTS

A SPECIAL THANK YOU
TO OUR INDIEGOGO SUPPORTERS:

Patty Flaherty Pagan
Shawna L Zak
Molly Yingling

GREAT THANKS TO OUR READERS:

Cassandra Rose Clarke
Morgan Cronin
Tyler Darnell
Esmeralda Fisher
Heather Gaff Mewis

Special acknowledgement is owed to Layla Al-Bedawi,
for coming up with the title and theme of this anthology,
and for always challenging the mind of the editor.

ABOUT WRITESPACE

Writespace is Houston's new writing center. Founded in April of 2014, we are a grassroots literary arts organization founded by writers, for writers. At Writespace, we support writers of all genres, including writers of literary fiction, poetry, science-fiction, fantasy, mystery, young adult, and other genres. Through our weekly writing workshops led by some of Houston's finest writing teachers, we seek to give writers who can't afford to earn an MFA in Creative Writing the same high-quality training and mentorship opportunities available through MFA programs.

As well as hosting workshops, Writespace offers manuscript consultations, write-ins, readings and open mics, and classes and private lessons for young writers. At Writespace, we plan to have such a positive impact on the local and the global writing community that great books that weren't going to be written will now be written.

Visit our website: www.writespacehouston.org.

ABOUT THE COVER ARTIST

John Bernhard is a Swiss American artist, photographer and writer who traveled North America extensively before settling in Houston, Texas in 1980. For more than three decades he has chosen the medium of photography to explore the everyday world from new perspectives, breaking away into different pathways of artistic expression. He continues to devote all of his energy taking photographs and bringing them together to enhance their meaning with visual interplay.

Bernhard was educated at the EPSIC Technical College in Lausanne and at the Ecole des Arts Decoratifs de Geneve in Switzerland. He is the author of 9 books among which are: *Nudes Metamorphs, Nicaragua, Diptych, Evanescence, Drift, China,* and his most recent monograph *Body Work*, a thirty years retrospective of photographs of the Nudes. In 2011 Bernhard's first non-fiction book, *America's Call,* was published by Dog Ear Publishing. In 2013 the french version, *L'Appel de L'Amérique,* illustrated with 57 color photographs and collages was published by Infolio Edition, Switzerland.

Beginning in 1985 with a solo exhibition at the Houston Center for Photography, Bernhard has had more than 30 solo shows, three museum exhibitions, and many collective exhibitions throughout the U.S., Canada, and Europe.

Bernhard's photographs are also included in 20 museum's permanent collection, such as the Denver Museum of Art, Minneapolis Institute of the Arts, Musée de la Photographie, Belgium, Musée de L'Elysée, Switzerland, Museet for Fotokunst, Denmark, New Mexico Museum of Arts, Pushkin Museum of Art, Russia, Southeast Museum of Photography, Florida, and The Museum of Fine Arts, Houston. His art has been collected by Texas Tech University, International Cultural Center ICASALS, and the Harry Ransom Humanities Research Center at the University of Texas. In 2001 is work was exhibited in *Body Work* curated by Christian Peterson, a 120 year survey of photographs of the nude selected from the permanent collection of the Minneapolis Institute of Arts. In 2004 his work was exhibited as a retrospective at the Musée des Suisses dans le Monde in Geneva, Switzerland. His children's portrait series Blue Marble made its debut with a solo exhibition at Rice University, Houston in 2011 and was featured on Artist A Day, and was awarded third prize in the 2014 Prix de la Photographie Paris.

Bernhard's work has been reviewed in publications such as *Communication Arts, Graphis, Photo District New Magazine, The Houston Chronicle, ArtSpeak Magazine, Swiss Review*, and has been widely published in such books as *Love & Desire* by William A. Ewing, (*Chronicle Books*), *Female Contemporary Nude Photography III*, (*UDYAT*), Spain, and *Nude Bible*, (Tectum Publishers, Belgium).

Find him online at: http://www.johnbernhard.net/